W9-CON-164

SUPER SANTA
The Science of Christmas

Written by **Bruce Hale**   Illustrated by **Guy Francis**

HARPER

An Imprint of HarperCollinsPublishers

Super Santa: The Science of Christmas

Copyright © 2021 by HarperCollins Publishers

All rights reserved. Manufactured in Italy.

No part of this book may be used or reproduced in any manner whatsoever without written permission except in the case of brief quotations embodied in critical articles and reviews. For information address HarperCollins Children's Books, a division of HarperCollins Publishers, 195 Broadway, New York, NY 10007.

www.harpercollinschildrens.com

ISBN 978-0-06-298363-3

The artist used software to manipulate the composite photographs for this book.

Typography by Rachel Zegar

21 22 23 24 25   RTLO   10 9 8 7 6 5 4 3 2 1

❖

First Edition

For Daryl, with thanks for all the math-and-sciencey goodness
—B.H.

To my elves: Calvin, Elle, Sammy, Mattie, and Max
—G.F.

Hey-ho, here we go!

It's countdown time—just minutes away from Christmas Eve, the most magical night of the year. Let's take a peek behind the scenes to see how things are going in Santa's workshop. . . .

All year long, we elves have been hustling and bustling, making presents for all the good boys and girls around the world. How many presents?

Well, Santa visits about 200 million homes on Christmas (depending on who's been naughty or nice), and if you figure two nice kids per house getting three presents each—jumpin' Jack Frost! That's over a billion presents. Line them up and they could stretch three times around the Earth.

Luckily, Santa has designed his workshop to handle this crazy workload.

In the garage, Mrs. Claus and her team are double-checking Santa's sled. This isn't some dime-a-dozen toboggan. Tonight, it'll travel about 20 million miles. That's like flying to the moon and back five times. It would take Superman more than a year to deliver all the presents that Santa does in one night.

But then when you pile on all the presents—holy holly berries! Even if the average gift weighs as much as a Lego set (about two pounds), the sleigh will have to carry more than a million tons. It's like Santa's carrying around three Empire State Buildings in his little red sled.

But what's really amazing is that even at that speed, with all that weight, the whole sled still can safely come to a stop—bibbedy-bop!—in the space of a single roof. Santa's crew spends weeks tuning up the brakes and making sure the reindeer's hooves are super-duper nonskid. At the North Pole, we don't take any chances when it comes to everyone's safety!

Hey-ho, oh no! It's almost go time, but before he takes off, we have to help Santa into his suit. At the speeds he'll be traveling, things get mighty toasty, and the compression is out of this world.

That's why St. Nick's suit has to be super-specially designed! It needs to handle all the heat and pressure that comes with such high-speed travel.

And speaking of pressure, Santa had better get a move on or he won't be able to deliver all the presents before sunrise!

Ka-chunga-chonk!

Uh-oh! The conveyor belt's jammed. All elves on deck! Looks like too many kids were nice this year. Suffering snowballs! What'll we do?

In the thick of it all, Santa and Mrs. Claus stay cool. She leads the loading while Santa makes sure the presents are all strapped on tight. But we're almost a half hour behind schedule now. How will he ever make up all that time?

Three . . . two . . . one . . . *Kat-choom!*

Hey-ho, away they go, in a sprinkle of stardust and snowflakes. As the sleigh leaves, the big guy winks, as if to say, "All will be well." Will he go fast enough? Will the sleigh hold up under all the weight? Will he be able to hit the brakes perfectly on every rooftop? Don't worry. We all know he will. Santa has it all figured out. Kris Kringle is a Christmas superhero!

What a takeoff! Santa and his reindeer zoom away at 730,000 miles
per hour. That's how fast the sled has to go to reach every house in time.

If you were to accelerate as fast as Santa does, the g-forces would make it feel like there were seventeen blue whales on top of you! But for Santa in his super suit, it's no big thing at all.

To make up for lost time, Santa puts his super smarts to work again. By flying from east to west across the international date line, he's able to turn Christmas Eve into thirty-one hours of darkness for his deliveries.

In fact, he's doing so well that Santa has time to chow down 400 million cookies and drink almost 200 million glasses of milk. Taken together, that's enough calories in one night to keep someone going for years. But Santa needs every last bite. Delivering this many presents is hard work!

As the sun peeks over the horizon, here come sleepy-eyed Santa, nine tired reindeer, and one empty sleigh. Jangling jingle bells—it's been another exhausting but successful Christmas Eve!

Hey-ho, what do you know? Bet you never thought that Santa was a Christmas superhero! It's all part of this special day's sparkle. But none of it would be possible without a little science and engineering and a whole lot of Christmas magic.

So when you're opening that perfect gift on Christmas morning, pause for a moment. Think about everything that Santa has done to put a present in your hands and send up a thank-you to super St. Nick, Mrs. Claus's can-do attitude, and the most tech-savvy team of elves in the whole North Pole.

Merry Christmas!